COMING HOME
A HOPI RESISTANCE STORY

TUTUQAYKINGAQW NIMA
HOPISINO PAHAN TUTQAYIWUY EP YORHOMTI

MAVASTA HONYOUTI
HOPI TRANSLATION BY MARILYN PARRA

LEVINE QUERIDO

Montclair | Amsterdam | Hoboken

When I was a boy, I would go with my kwa'a to our cornfield. He would pick me up early in the morning and we would drive in his white pickup truck on a dusty road, listening to old country songs on the radio. When we got there, he would pick a watermelon and bury it in the sand. I would help him by hoeing the weeds or thinning the plants. It was hot and boring to me, so I would work for a while then take long breaks. I think I would have rather thrown rocks into the wash or sat under the shade of the tailgate. But whenever I would glance over at my kwa'a, he would be on his hands and knees, crawling to the next plant, taking care of each individual stalk.

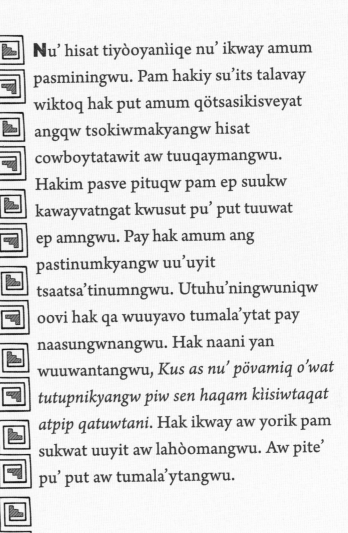

Nu' hisat tiyòoyanìiqe nu' ikway amum pasminingwu. Pam hakiy su'its talavay wiktoq hak put amum qötsasikisveyat angqw tsokiwmakyangw hisat cowboytatawit aw tuuqaymangwu. Hakim pasve pituqw pam ep suukw kawayvatngat kwusut pu' put tuuwat ep amngwu. Pay hak amum ang pastinumkyangw uu'uyit tsaatsa'tinumngwu. Utuhu'ningwuniqw oovi hak qa wuuyavo tumala'ytat pay naasungwnangwu. Hak naani yan wuuwantangwu, *Kus as nu' pövamiq o'wat tutupnikyangw piw sen haqam kìisiwtaqat atpip qatuwtani.* Hak ikway aw yorik pam sukwat uuyit aw lahòomangwu. Aw pite' pu' put aw tumala'ytangwu.

Finally, he would take a break.
At lunchtime we would have piki,
crackers, sardines, fruit, or Vienna
sausages. Then he would dig out
the watermelon from the ground,
crack it on the tailgate of his truck,
and use his thumbnail to split the
melon.

Nawis'ew pam naasungwnangwu.
Taawanasave hakim piikitnit,
pölavik'lakpuhòoyatnit, paakiwsikwitnit,
natwanitnit pu' piw mumriwput
sisikwiwhòoyat nösngwu. Pàasat pu' pam
kawayvatngat ep hangwat pu' put
tsìikyaknangwu. Pam wukomlatsiy
sokiyat akw kawayvatngat naaho
kwanaknangwu.

I was always amazed at how my kwa'a used his nails for tools. He would often take out a piece of paako too and use his pocket knife to whittle away. He made wood carvings that I later learned to do myself.

Sometimes, I would wonder what my kwa'a was like when he was my age.

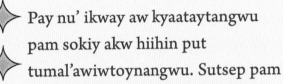
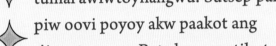
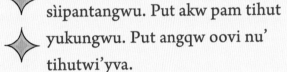

Pay nu' ikway aw kyaataytangwu pam sokiy akw hiihin put tumal'awiwtoynangwu. Sutsep pam piw oovi poyoy akw paakot ang sìipantangwu. Put akw pam tihut yukungwu. Put angqw oovi nu' tihutwi'yva.

Pay ephaqamtöqw hak yan wuuwantangwu, *Sen ikwa hisat inun tsayni'yqe hintangwu?*

It wasn't until later that I heard the story of when my kwa'a was a boy, when he was taken from his family to a school far away. His parents hid him from the government agents when they rounded up children in the village. He could hear the officers' voices from underneath the pile of blankets and sheep skins.

Pay pas hisattiqw nu' navót yaw ikwa tiyòoyaniqw put yaw haqami yaavok tutuqaykit aqw wikya. Put yaw yumat Kàvument solaawamuy amungaqw tupkya. Solaawam yaw kitsokiyamuy ang tsaatsakmuy tsovalantinumya. Tatvupputnit kanelvuvukyat tutukmol'iwtaqat atpipaqe pakiwkyangw yaw pam solaawamuy susmataqw yu'a'atotaqw nanvotngwu.

But his dad was threatened with arrest. Just like the other Hopi men who had resisted a generation prior and were taken as prisoners to Alcatraz.

Ikway nayat yaw solaawam tsatsawinaya put ngu'aye' yaw panayaniqey yan aw hingqaqwa. Pay hin hisat ura Hopi tàataqtuy rohòmtotiqamuy anum'i. Pumuy ura ngu'atotat haqami Alcatraz aqw tsamyaqe pepehaqw pumuy sivatangatota.

Eventually they found my kwa'a and took him. He was put on a wagon with other Hopi children that he knew. It was early morning and the ride was long and bumpy.

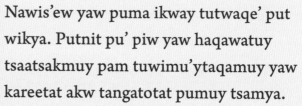

Nawis'ew yaw puma ikway tutwaqe' put wikya. Putnit pu' piw yaw haqawatuy tsaatsakmuy pam tuwimu'ytaqamuy yaw kareetat akw tangatotat pumuy tsamya. Su'its talavay yaw pumuy tsamya.

The children were taken to a place called Keams Canyon, fifty miles from their village. All of them were gathered in a large room. Some they sent to get their hair cut, while others were brought to a room where they were plunged into a smelly fluid. Everyone was made to put new clothes on.

Pongsikmiq yaw tsaatsakmuy tsamya.
Pumuy kitsoki'am yaw pangqw yaavo.
Pumuy yaw haqami suukw
wuko'àapavi'ytaqat aw tangatota.
Haqawatuy yaw haqamiwat hoonayaqe'
pep pumuy aarilaya. Pu' piw yaw
haqawatuy haqamiwat tangatotaqey pep
pumuy hìita ani hin hovaqtuqat
kuuyiwtaqat aqw pumuy yòotsikintota.
Sòosokmuy tsaatsakmuy yaw ayatota
puma puhuyuwsit ang ungniqat.

Next, they separated the boys into one line and the girls into another. They were led into a room with large blackboards in the front, covered in various names. Each child was instructed to select a name that was to become their new one. But when asked, my kwa'a said he already had a name. He was named by his paternal grandmother when he was only twenty days old. His name was Honkuku, meaning Bear's Paw. The man replied simply, "Now, you must choose a new name."

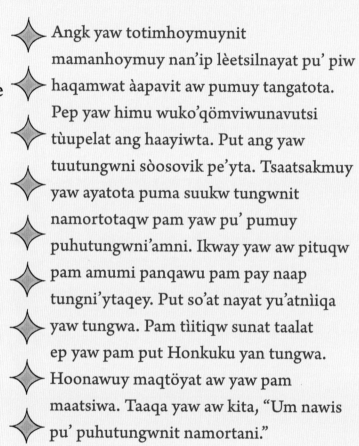

Angk yaw totimhoymuynit mamanhoymuy nan'ip lèetsilnayat pu' piw haqamwat àapavit aw pumuy tangatota. Pep yaw himu wuko'qömviwunavutsi tùupelat ang haayiwta. Put ang yaw tuutungwni sòosovik pe'yta. Tsaatsakmuy yaw ayatota puma suukw tungwnit namortotaqw pam yaw pu' pumuy puhutungwni'amni. Ikway yaw aw pituqw pam amumi panqawu pam pay naap tungni'ytaqey. Put so'at nayat yu'atnìiqa yaw tungwa. Pam tìitiqw sunat taalat ep yaw pam put Honkuku yan tungwa. Hoonawuy maqtöyat aw yaw pam maatsiwa. Taaqa yaw aw kita, "Um nawis pu' puhutungwnit namortani."

My kwa'a looked at all the names on the board but he didn't recognize what they were. All the writing was new to him: everyone that he knew had a Hopi name, but they were never written, only spoken. Finally, a name did catch his eye: Clyde. He pointed, and the man nodded his head and wrote it in a book. The man said it was a good Christian name. Then the man asked Clyde once again what his "Indian name" was. Clyde said once more: Honkuku. The man looked puzzled at first, then wrote something in his book. He handed Clyde a name card which he was to wear around his neck. It read: Clyde Honyouti.

Ikwa yaw sòosok tuutungwnit ang yori. Niikyangw yaw qa hìitawat maamatsi. Kur himu yaw ang pe'yyungwa. Paypi as yaw sòosoyam naap Hopitungwni'yyungwa. Niikyangw pam qa peeniwtangwu panis yu'a'atiwa. Nawis'ew yaw suukya tungwni angqw aw maataqti-Clyde. Pam yaw malatsiy akw aw maamasa. Taaqa yaw aw yokokoykut pu' tutuvenit ang tungwnit peena. Taaqa yaw aw pangqawu i' tungwni yaw pas lomatsiisas tungwni. Taaqa yaw Clyde piw tuuvingta hin pam yotamaatsiwqw. Piw yaw aw kita, "Honkuku." Taaqa yaw aw hin yorit pu' piw tutuvenit ang hìita peena. Pàasat yaw taaqa Clyde aw tutuvenhoyat tavi. Ang yaw Clyde Honyouti pe'yta. Put yaw pam ngönnumni.

Clyde and all of the other children with new names missed their homes and their parents. It was a scary place. Whenever one of the children would speak Hopi, they would get punished.

Clydeniqw tsaatsayom pu' puhutungwni'yvayaqam yaw yumuynit kiikiy sölmokiwyungwa. Pas yaw puma haqam maqas'eway epehaqya. Son yaw himuwa tsay Hopiyu'a'aykungwu pay yaw piw put sivintonayangwu.

So, they whispered to each other instead. At night, the smaller kids would cry and the older kids would comfort them.

 Nawus yaw puma naanami na'uyu'a'atotangwu. Mihiqw yaw tsaatsayom tsaykitangwu. Pu' yaw wungwiwyungqam pumuy amumi unangtavi'yyungngwu.

Clyde did what he was told, but he knew he wanted to be back home. He decided he would never let anyone take his language and love for his culture away from him. And so, early one morning, he and his friend tried to run away. They got a few miles down the road, but a man on a horse caught them and brought them back to the school. The boys were whipped for trying to escape.

Pay yaw as Clyde sölmokiwtakyangw pay nawus yaw hin aw tutaplalwaqw pam pantingwu. Hisat yaw su'its talavay pamiqw kwaatsi'at waaya. Pay yaw puma naat qa pas yaavo pituq pay hak taaqa kawayot akw tsokiwmaqa puma amungk pitut pu' pumuy ahoy tutuqaykimi wiiki. Puma yaw wuvàatiwa ispi puma yaw waayaniqey tuwanta.

Another time, they tried to return home but didn't take the road, instead climbing the rocks above the school. It was hot and they were thirsty.

The boys had forgotten to grab food and water before they left. The school was many miles away from their village, and it would take several days to get there. So, they decided it would be better to go back. Of course, they got punished again.

Time went by, and things did get easier. Clyde did the work he was instructed to do. Eventually, he learned to read and write in English.

Piw yaw puma hisat tuwanta nimaniqey. Puma yaw pay qa pöhut angnit yaw tuwat haqe' owaqwlöt ang wuuvi. Pas yaw utuhu'niqw puma hikwmoki.

Tiyot yaw kur sùutoki nöösiwqatnit kuuyit nàasataniqey. Pumuy kitsoki'am tutuqaykinaqw yaavoniqw oovi yaw pas sonqa löös taalat ang puma aqw pituni. Pay yaw puma oovi naami yan yuku ahoy tutuqaykiminiqey. Antsa pay yaw piw pumuy sivintoyna puma ahoy aw pitunqw.

Haqàapi yaw Clyde engem pay pu' himu qa pas hinta. Pay hìita hin aw tutaplalwaqw pam pan tumala'ytangwu. Nawis'ew yaw pam tungwantuwi'yva piw pentuwi'yva.

And finally, he was allowed to return home. Nawis'ew yaw put nakwhanaya pam nimaniniqw.

Clyde told his parents what had happened at that school. They were happy he was back home. They told him all that had gone on in the village, the ceremonies he had missed, and how things had changed while he was away.

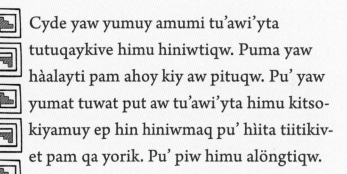

Cyde yaw yumuy amumi tu'awi'yta tutuqaykive himu hiniwtiqw. Puma yaw hàalayti pam ahoy kiy aw pituqw. Pu' yaw yumat tuwat put aw tu'awi'yta himu kitso-kiyamuy ep hin hiniwmaq pu' hìita tiitikiv-et pam qa yorik. Pu' piw himu alöngtiqw.

My kwa'a went through a lot when he was at that school. Later in his years, he chose a much simpler life: a farmer's life. He enjoyed his time in his field and he took great care for his plants, just like he took great care of his family.

Now all his children, grandchildren, and great-grandchildren have his last name: Honyouti. Our name was changed by his time at that school, but it still has meaning. It means a pack of bears that are running together.

Ikwa yaw tutuqaykive hiihìita ang kuyva. Pas yaw asòntiqw pam sus'qahintaqat qatsit namorta, Pasvanìiqat qatsit. Pam oovi pasva tumal'ytangwuni'yqe pas yaw put akw naavokyawintima. Pu' piw uu'uyiy pas amumi tunatyawtangwu pay timuy amuni.

Yan haqam oovi ikway timatniqw mömat pu' put tungwniyat himu'yyungwa. - Honyouti. Yan haqam oovi piw itàakway tungwni'at tutuqaykive alöngti. Niikyangw pay naat pam pas hìita tu'awi'yta. Pam it tu'awi'yta- Hoohont naanama yùutukiwmaqat.

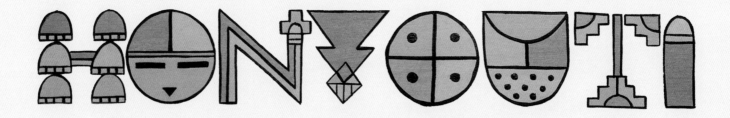

I always felt like I had a special relationship with my kwa'a. He taught me lessons that I didn't understand as a kid, but they made sense when I became an adult. When I get to difficult times, I remember him.

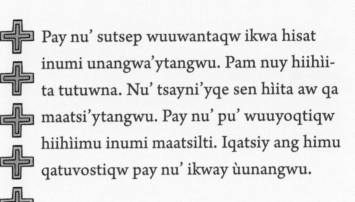

Pay nu' sutsep wuuwantaqw ikwa hisat inumi unangwa'ytangwu. Pam nuy hiihìi-ta tutuwna. Nu' tsayni'yqe sen hìita aw qa maatsi'ytangwu. Pay nu' pu' wuuyoqtiqw hiihìimu inumi maatsilti. Iqatsiy ang himu qatuvostiqw pay nu' ikway ùunangwu.

A NOTE ON HISTORY AND LEARNING

In times before the government came to our people, Hopi children learned everything from their families and community members. They were closely involved in daily activities and participated in various ceremonies. Teaching and knowledge were passed on to the younger ones through language in stories, songs, and games. Older children helped their parents in their homes and in the fields. Knowledge was everywhere.

When the boarding schools were established, everything changed. Children were taken from their families and villages. They were not allowed to speak their language and were punished if they did. They were told what to do and were afraid of the adults in charge. The parents were threatened with arrest if they refused to send their kids to school—and in 1895, a group of nineteen Hopi men were sent to Alcatraz to show others what might happen to them if they continued to resist. Those changes caused a lot of damage. It took a long time for families to recover from the boarding school era. There was a separation between parents, children, and their communities.

The US and Canadian governments echoed these practices across North America from the late nineteenth century well into the twentieth century. In hundreds of residential boarding schools, some run by the government and some by churches, hundreds of thousands of Native children were taken from their homes with the goal of assimilating them into mainstream culture—"to kill the Indian in him, and save the man." In addition to losing connection to their culture, language, homeland, and families, many Native children also died at the schools from disease, malnutrition, or abuse. They did not make it home.

The Hopi men who were imprisoned at Alcatraz for resisting government efforts to send their children to boarding school. From the Mennonite Library and Archives, Bethel College.

We Hopi, like many other tribes, are now in a time of healing and revitalization. Families and communities are rebuilding relationships. School is not a place of separation and intimidation anymore. Many community schools are teaching the Hopi language to increase fluent speakers. The culture is alive and thriving. Even though it was threatened with extinction, our people never let it go. Language and knowledge is still being passed on to the younger generations. It is a challenge, but the work is happening to save what we have.

A NOTE ON THE TRANSLATION

Mrs. Parra translated this story. She teaches the Hopilavayi (Hopi language) to our children. Her work is so valuable in the way she keeps our language alive. In the past, the educational system was designed to destroy our way of life, but it was unsuccessful. I became a teacher just like many family members, and I fully understand my position and role as an educator. I am able to instruct my students to use education as a tool, or secret weapon, to navigate through the ever-changing world and to always protect what we love. Our ancestors were taught to be warriors; I am preparing our children to be Intellectual Warriors.

—Mavasta Honyouti

My children and I in our family's field.

Hopilavayi—Hopi language—is an ancient language of the Hopi Pueblo people of Northeastern Arizona. It is a language that has been passed down orally from generation to generation since time immemorial. Hopilavayi is the only Pueblo language in Arizona that belongs to the Uto-Aztecan language family. There are three dialects of Hopilavayi: First Mesa, Second Mesa and Third Mesa. First Mesa consists of these three villages: Walpi, Sitsomovi, and Hanoki. Second Mesa villages are: Songòopavi, Musangnuvi, and Supawlavi. Orayvi, Kiqötsmovi, Ho'atvela, Paaqavi, and Mùnqapi are Third Mesa villages. The three mesas are located on the Colorado Plateau Region in the Four Corners area of the Southwest, which is the states of Arizona, New Mexico, Colorado, and Utah.

Although Hopilavayi is still spoken by the elders and individuals who are sixty-plus years of age, the younger generation of Hopi children are speaking less and less Hopilavayi. The diminishing usage of the language is due to Western education and exposure to the mainstream society-Pahànqatsi-Anglo way of life. The preservation of our language is currently being addressed by the Hopi people and it is being taught throughout the local elementary schools and at the high school. The survival of our centuries-old language is crucial to the continuation of our Hopi Way of Life—Hopiqatsi.

As a translator for this story—*Coming Home*—I was deeply touched by how Mavasta brought me back in time to our grandparents and great-grandparents' times, when they were forcefully taken away from their parents and their villages to be educated in an unfamiliar place and in a language that was foreign to them. These types of stories touch me so deeply because I was born and raised in the oldest continuously inhabited village of the United States—Orayvi (Old Oraibi). Many of the Hopi children were taken from this specific village as told by our family members. I myself experienced having to be sent off to a boarding school off the reservation. However, it was a different type of experience for me. It was a choice that all Hopi families were given for the reason that there were no high schools on our reservation at the time.

Upon my return back to my home village in 1997, having lived away from my reservation for twenty-plus years, I took up the interest of learning to read and write our language. My journey began by attending the first ever Hopi Teacher Training on Reading and Writing in Hopi, with the late Emory Sekyaquaptewa. He became my mentor before his time of passing. Emory worked on developing the *Hopìikwa Lavàytutuveni—Hopi Dictionary* during his tenure at the University of Arizona in Tucson. This dictionary is an invaluable tool for reading and writing in Hopilavayi. As I create my lessons for teaching Hopilavayi or writing, I refer to this document to justify the correct spelling of words, pronunciation, word meaning, and sentence usage.

Marilyn and I together, outside the school we teach in.

With the Third Mesa dialect, which I am a speaker of and where Mavasta is from as well, it is important to ensure that the different markings for vowel glides and the glottal stops are correct, for they are unique to that specific dialect. Another consideration is gender speech. Specifically for the Third Mesa dialect, there are some words that are used only by females and vice versa by males. As an example, for the word for "thank you," females will say "Askwali" and males will say "Kwakwha." While working on the book, as a female translator, I paid special attention to words specifically used by male speakers. Furthermore, writing as a second speaker, I used the word "yaw" throughout. This word means "for it is told."

My Hopi name is Qoyawisnöm—Gray Dawn Stretched About. This name was given to me by my godmother at the time of my initiation into the Katsina Society when I was about twelve years old. This name comes from the Sun Clan. I am a member of the Young Corn Clan—Piikyaswungwa. My English name is Marilyn Parra, and I teach Hopilavayi at one of our local elementary schools.

A NOTE ON MY ART

Wood carving has been a family tradition for generations. Hopi wood carving is a traditional art form that has evolved over time and is collected all over the world. I began to carve around the age of fifteen. My first teacher was my father, Ron Honyouti, who learned from his own father (my kwa'a) and his older brother, Brian. My dad would allow me to finish pieces that he started. He guided me along the way with new techniques and implementing movement, anatomy, and details. I grew up attending art shows with him and my uncles too, so I had the opportunity to see other art forms and mediums. To this day, I have been inspired by the creativity of other artists.

Over time, I developed my own style of carving. The work featured in this story is done using a relief carving technique. I was inspired by Egyptian reliefs, classical statues, and Mayan codices and applied it to my work.

The material I use is cottonwood root, or paako. It is lightweight and fairly easy to carve if your tools are sharp. For this book, the wood was hand-cut into planks and then the carving of the art began. My tools are chisels, gouges, and knives in different sizes. I also use a woodburner tool to make details like textures on fabrics, outlines, and hair. The pieces are painted with a thin layer of acrylic paint. I prefer light and earth tones in my finished pieces.

My kwa'a, carving.

My workspace.

1. *The tools my dad gave me on my 18th birthday, which I still use.*

2. *My daughter's toy that she left among my tools.*

3. *The desk my uncle made for me when I was a child, which I still use.*

5. *Carving completed.*

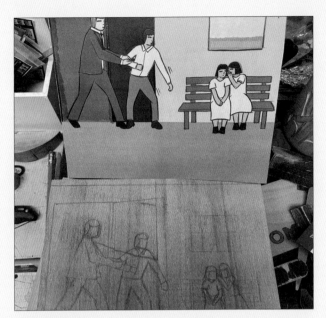

4. Initial sketches.

6. Finishing up!

This is for the children who made it home.
And for those who did not.

My kwa'a

This is an Arthur A. Levine book
Published by Levine Querido

LQ
LEVINE QUERIDO

www.levinequerido.com · info@levinequerido.com

Levine Querido is distributed by Chronicle Books, LLC

Text and art copyright © 2024 by Mavasta Honyouti
Hopi translation copyright © 2024 by Marilyn Parra
Art photography by Addison Doty

Library of Congress Control Number: 2023951115
ISBN 978-1-64614-457-0

Printed and bound in China

MIX
Paper | Supporting
responsible forestry
FSC™ C008047
FSC
www.fsc.org

Published in November 2024
First Printing

The text was set in Arno Pro
Book design by Jennifer Browne